Birdie

Birdie

by
Eileen Spinelli

Eerdmans Books for Young Readers

Grand Rapids, Michigan

Text © 2019 Eileen Spinelli

Published in 2019 by Eerdmans Books for Young Readers,
an imprint of Wm. B. Eerdmans Publishing Co.
Grand Rapids, Michigan

www.eerdmans.com/youngreaders

26 25 24 23 22 21 20 19   1 2 3 4 5 6 7 8 9

Library of Congress Cataloging-in-Publication Data

Names: Spinelli, Eileen, author.
Title: Birdie / Eileen Spinelli.
Description: Grand Rapids, MI : Eerdmans Books for Young Readers, 2019. |
  Summary: Still grieving for her father, twelve-year-old Birdie struggles
  to adjust to many changes, including when her grandmother, her mother, and
  her best friends all begin dating.
Identifiers: LCCN 2018038702 | ISBN 9780802855138 (hardback)
Subjects: | CYAC: Novels in verse. | Family life—Fiction. |
  Friendship—Fiction. | Dating (Social customs)—Fiction. | Grief—Fiction.
  | Single-parent families—Fiction. | BISAC: JUVENILE FICTION / Stories in
  Verse. | JUVENILE FICTION / Social Issues / Adolescence. | JUVENILE
  FICTION / Family / Multigenerational.
Classification: LCC PZ7.5.S68 Bir 2019 | DDC [Fic]—dc23 LC record available at
https://lccn.loc.gov/2018038702

Cover illustration © 2019 Vivian Mineker

For Roman and Isabella and for Savannah and Miriam
and Dominic Jerry, new to the family nest, and also for
birdies Alana and Elliott, Greyson and Nora.

— *E. S.*

feathery

I pick the hairs
from my brush.
I put them in
my pocket.
I will drop them
on the grass
on my way to
Mrs. Bloom's.

I do this
every Saturday.

As a kid,
I told my mom
I wanted to be a bird
when I grew up.
She never said
I couldn't.
So for years
I bird-sang my words.
And saved dryer lint
and old gift ribbons
for future nests.

I flapped my arms
when I walked.
And more than once
Mom had to
clean my right ear—
the one I would put
to the ground to
listen for worms.

Of course now
that I'm twelve,
I realize how silly
all that was.

Still—there is something
light and feathery
in my heart
at the idea
that a bird
may be weaving
the hairs from my brush
into its nest.

unofficially

I read everything
I can about birds.
I love watching them.
I learn their songs.
I keep bird charts
in my room.
I use my allowance
to buy birdseed
for our backyard feeders.
And then
there is my name.
My birth certificate says
I'm Roberta Briggs.
But the minute I turn eighteen,
I'm changing it to Birdie Briggs.
Officially.
For now
Birdie (unofficially)
is what everyone
calls me.

seasoning

There is no public library
in Hadley Falls.
The nearest one
is in Gillette—
three towns away.
So Mrs. Bloom
has turned five shelves
of her pantry
into a lending library.
I'm returning
a book for Maymee:
Backstage Murders.
The pages still smell
like Mrs. Bloom's garlic powder.

next book

Mrs. Bloom takes
Backstage Murders
and hands me
Murder at Midnight.
"Maymee will like this one,"

she says. "It takes place
in a cemetery."
We both smile.
My grandma, Maymee,
has been planning her funeral
for the last three years.
Maymee says it gives her
a reason to
get up in the morning.

painted toes

Nina Faull, who
lives next door to Mrs. Bloom,
is sitting on her front step
painting her toenails
bright purple.
She wags the bottle
of polish at me.
"You're next!"
"Can't," I tell her.
"Maymee's waiting
for her book."

new

Nina is new in Hadley Falls.
She moved here from Idaho with her dad
and her little brother, Sammy.
When Nina told me
where she was from,
I told her
that the state bird of Idaho
is the mountain bluebird.
She was *very* impressed.

more about nina

Nina wears at least
one purple thing
every day.
She dots her i's
with tiny hearts.
She likes talking about
boys.
Our first ride on
the school bus,
she told me about

her first kiss.
She was ten.
The boy was eleven.
It happened at
the Idaho State Fair
behind the booth selling
baked potato ice cream.
The boy's name was Bear.
He had been helping
his uncle at the booth
and was taking a break.
When Nina walked by,
he told her
she was the prettiest girl
in all of Idaho.
"Then he asked if he could kiss me."
Nina giggled. "What could
I say?"

idaho

All that day
my never-been-kissed head
was spinning.

A boy named Bear.
That boy asking
a complete stranger
for a kiss.
The stranger
saying yes.
Not to mention
baked potato ice cream!
Who knew
Idaho was so
exciting?

nicer

When I get home
from Mrs. Bloom's,
Maymee is standing
on the porch
in her bathrobe,
waving a book-looking
something
at me.
It's an undertaker's catalog.
"Birdie," she says. "Look!"

I found a nicer coffin.
A blue one.
It will go better with
my blue polka-dot dress."

plans so far

Last year
Maymee wanted to be buried
in her pink suit.
But then a new donut shop
opened in Hadley Falls,
and Maymee gained eight pounds
and outgrew the suit.
Flowers?
Lilies and yellow roses.
She has chosen one hymn
so far:
"All of Us Go Down to the Dust,"
which I found for her online.
She was so grateful
that she wrote me into her will.
I get her egg cup collection.

what about mozart

I had another funeral idea:
starlings.
Starlings are fairly common.
A lot of people don't like them.
But I do.
So did Mozart, the famous composer.
He kept a starling as a pet.
He wove the starling's song
into his own compositions.
When his starling died,
Mozart gave it a fancy funeral.
"Have the organist
play Mozart, Maymee," I suggested.
"And get the undertaker
to release a swirl of starlings
over your grave."
Maymee gave that idea
a thumbs-down.
"Too hoity-toity," she said.

leaving philadelphia

Mom and I came to Hadley Falls
from Philadelphia
soon after my dad died
in the line of duty.
Three years ago.
Dad was a firefighter.
He had gone into
an old, rotting warehouse
that was in flames.
His buddy, Jamar, told Mom
that Dad went in because
he was worried there might be
homeless people living
in the building.
There were not.
Just a bunch of old paint cans
and rags and trash.

After the fire,
Mom said living in the city
was too sad.
And too expensive.
So we came to Hadley Falls,

a hundred miles away,
to move in with Maymee.
It's cheaper for us.
And less lonely for Maymee.
"Win-win,"
Maymee says.

late again

Mom works at the Redbud Diner.
Her hours are usually 8 a.m. to 3 p.m.
Around 1:30 she calls.
"Birdie, honey, I'm going to be home late."
"How late?" I ask.
"Around six. Errands and stuff."
When I hang up, Maymee gives me a look.
"She's going to be late, right? Again."
"Errands and stuff," I say.
Maymee snorts.
"Errands my patootie."

silly

Mom got a new computer.
She's thinking of going to
online college
for practical nursing.
Maymee says
online dating
is more like it.
I say that's silly.
Mom loved Dad too much.
Besides—
she has me
to keep her from
being lonely.

martin stefano

At two o'clock
Martin Stefano comes by
for our Saturday Scrabble game.
Martin was the first friend I made
when we moved to Hadley Falls.
That summer he showed me

around town:
the creek, the park, the Dollar Store.
He also got me invited
to Charlie Deale's
Lego-themed birthday party—
Lego-shaped cake,
Lego scavenger hunt.
We even got to help Charlie
build a Lego marble run.
Half of Charlie's room was
filled with Lego sets.
Still is.

When school started,
Martin showed me how to get to our classroom,
and the cafeteria,
and the nurse's office.
He told me that our teacher,
Ms. Portage,
was the one with the red hair,
the clumpy earrings,
and the big smile.

He advised me to steer clear
of the tapioca pudding

at lunch.
"The rumor last year," he said,
"was that a mouse
drowned in it."

weekly game

I used to play
Scrabble
with my dad
every week.
On Saturdays.
And though I almost
never talk about Dad,
I did mention
those games
to Martin.
It was Martin's idea
to continue
the tradition.

no thanks

When Nina moved to Hadley Falls
we invited her to join us
for Scrabble.
She said: "Ugh. Word games are
bor-ing."

snack time

Usually Mom makes
our snacks for
Scrabble Saturday.
But she's going to be late,
so Maymee takes over.
She microwaves
a bag of popcorn.
She burns it.
So she gives us
two Fig Newtons
from her personal stash.
Martin and I
hate Fig Newtons.
But we have to

eat them
because Maymee
is watching us.

theme

To make our games
more challenging,
Martin and I do
themes.
Today it's Martin's choice.
He chooses "clothing."
He gets an *A* tile.
so he goes first.
T O G A.
I get a *Z*
two *U*s
B
T
R
and *E.*
I put down
the only clothing word
I can think of:

B R A.
Martin grins.
My face gets warm.
Dumb, I tell myself.
No need to be
embarrassed.
Martin is just a buddy.
Friend.
Pal.
Amigo.

everything is okay

Mom calls again.
At six.
"I'm on my way."
"Everything okay?" I ask.
"Everything's fine.
I just stopped for gas.
Can you make the salad?"
"Sure," I tell her,
and I stop worrying.

a lot better

For months
after Dad died,
I was a world-class
worrier.
I'd wake up
in the morning
with a knot in
my heart.
What if
Mom had died
during the night?
What if she slipped
in the shower
and hit her head?
What if she
touched a faulty wire
and got electrocuted?
All day
I'd drag around my
knotted-heart self.
Worrying.
Now things are better.
The knot is mostly gone.

Still—I can't help
wondering if
everything's okay
whenever she's
running late.

best

By the time Mom arrives
(with salmon loaf from work)
I have the salad made,
the table set
(on the porch because
it's warm for May,
and I like eating where
I can see birds),
the iced tea poured.
Mom hugs me.
She kisses the top
of my head.
"You," she says,
holding my face in
her hands, "are
the best."

company for dessert

We are just starting dessert—
ice cream sandwiches—
when Officer Downey appears.
He's waving a green-striped cane.
Maymee squeals. "My Tuesday cane!"
(Maymee has seven painted canes—
one for each day of the week.)
"Where did you find it?"
"At the drug store," he says.
Maymee tells me to get
an ice cream sandwich for
Officer Downey.
Mom says, "I'm sure Fred is busy."
"Fiddlesticks," says Maymee.
"Sit down, Fred."
Maymee has known Officer Downey
since he was in diapers.
(And thanks to her,
everybody in Hadley Falls
knows it.)
Officer Downey
sits.

birding

The four of us
eat our ice cream.
I point out
two goldfinches,
one chickadee,
and a blue jay.
Officer Downey
points to two geese.
He acts all proud.
I laugh.
Even Nina from Idaho
knows geese.

keeping her distance

Mom isn't talking much.
And I know why.
She's not about to
get too chummy
with Fred Downey.
It's because of his job.
His job puts him

in harm's way.
Every day.
Like Dad's job.
Once Aunt Louisa
tried to set Mom up
with a friend who was
a detective.
"Not interested," Mom told her.
"And if I were, it would be
in someone with a safe job.
Like a carpenter."

wavy

It's bedtime.
I mark my daily bird chart:
three starlings,
three crows,
two goldfinches,
one blue jay,
two geese,
one chickadee,
and one woodpecker.
(Which I heard but

didn't actually see.
Still, it counts.)

I put on my dad's
reading glasses.
I wear them
in my bedroom
every night.
The world is wavy
through them.
I sit on the edge of the bed
facing my window.
I look out at the bright wavy moon.

Once I saw
a wavy, moon-washed owl,
like in a picture book.
I believed the owl
was sent to me by my dad—
a gift that I could only see
when I wore
his glasses.

goodnight kisses

Mom comes in
to kiss me goodnight.
She checks my bird chart.
"No bluebirds today?" she says.
Mom loves bluebirds.
"Maybe tomorrow," I tell her.
After she leaves,
I lean over to pick up
the framed picture of my dad.
In it he's standing in our kitchen,
wearing his glasses,
studying a cookbook.
Mom told me he was
about to make an apple pie.
This is my favorite photo of him.
Every night
I pick up the photo and kiss it.
"Goodnight, Daddy," I say.

sunday morning

Sometimes I help Maymee
get ready for church.
She's perfectly capable,
but she dawdles.
I help her with her buttons
and her earrings.
I choose the shoes that
best match her outfit.
I do her makeup.
I tell Maymee,
"You don't need
too much.
Just a little lipstick."
"I'll be the judge of that,"
she says.

rushed

I button Maymee into
her yellow dress.
"This makes me look fat,"
she says.

I pull the dark-green dress
from her closet.
I help her into it.
She makes a face.
"My stomach looks
poofy."
I roll my eyes. "If you didn't
eat so many donuts . . . "
"Don't be rude, Birdie."
"I'm just saying . . . "
"Well—*don't* say."
She asks me to bring
her long silver beads,
"My poof won't
stand out so much
if I wear those."
Mom calls out:
"I'm leaving.
Ready or not!"
I grab my sweater.
Maymee grabs her Sunday cane—
painted pink flamingos.
Whew!
Ready.

angels

After Dad died,
I stopped going to church.
I blame Mrs. Wharton,
the head of the Ladies' Circle.
She told me that
God took Dad because
he needed another angel.
She said it thinking that
would comfort me.
I looked Mrs. Wharton
square in the eye
and said:
"Bull—if God
needed another angel,
he should have made
his own."

tattle-tale

Mrs. Wharton gave a gasp
and marched right up
to Mom at coffee hour.

She told Mom what
I had said.
"Brazen disrespect!"
Mrs. Wharton sniffed.
"Not only to me, but to God
as well."
It was Mom's turn to
look Mrs. Wharton square in the eye.
She said, "Surely God can handle
the broken heart of a nine-year-old."
And with that Mom took my hand
and we walked out.
"Mrs. Wharton is full of baloney,"
Mom told me on the way to the car.
"God didn't take Daddy.
The fire did."

the prodigal returns

I never went to
that church again.
And Mom didn't make me.
But when we moved to Hadley Falls,
the Hadley Grace Church hosted

an ice cream social.
With music and games
and all the sundae toppings
you could want.
I decided to give church—
and God—
a second chance.

who's that?

Mom sings in the Hadley Grace choir.
She sits in the choir loft.
Maymee and I head for
our usual seat six rows from the front.
Pastor Carey is halfway through
the Old Testament reading
when Maymee raises her cane
and points it at an older man
in the third row.
"Who's that?" she asks in a loud whisper.
"Shush," I tell her. "Everyone can hear you."
The man turns our way.
The pastor has stopped reading.
I want to disappear.

The man nods to Maymee. "I'm Harlan Gray."
"Are you new?" says Maymee.
She's not even whispering now.
Mr. Gray says: "I'm visiting my granddaughter
and her husband for the summer."
"Ahhh," says Maymee. "Well, welcome."
There is laughter in the pews.
Then clapping.
Maymee pokes me with her elbow.
She's all pleased with herself.
Pastor Carey smiles. "May I
resume the reading now?"

prayer request

During prayer requests,
Mavis Moon
asks for prayers
for her cat, Buzby,
who is sick.
Maymee shoots me a look.
(Maymee hates cats.)
I whisper: "Buzby is
one of God's creatures."

Maymee snorts.

"So is a bedbug."

cookies

Just before the sermon,
I leave for Sunday School.
Martin and Charlie are already there.
So is Loretta Lomax.
They're helping
our Sunday School teacher,
Mrs. Pinski, box cookies
for the people who can't
get out to church.
Mrs. Pinski reads
the three names
on this week's list:
"Mrs. Anderson. She had a baby
on Wednesday."
"Aww," says Loretta,
who loves babies. "I totally
want ten babies of my own."
"Moving along," says Mrs. Pinski,
"Mr. Kheen broke his toe.

And last—
Sammy Faull.
Nina Faull's little brother.
He has a cold."
This was my doing.
Nina's family aren't church members,
but I asked Mrs. Pinski
if we could add Sammy's name
to the list anyway.

assignments

We tie red ribbons
around the cookie boxes.
Mrs. Pinski gives Loretta
the box for the Andersons.
"I get to see the new baby!"
squeals Loretta.
"And Charlie," says Mrs. Pinksi,
"you can deliver your cookies
to Mr. Kheen."
Charlie Deale grumbles.
"Oh goody. I get to see
Mr. Kheen's big toe."

Mrs. Pinski wags her finger
at Charlie. "Be nice," she says.
Martin offers to take
Sammy's.
"I'll come along," I say.
"That's okay, Birdie," says Martin.
"You don't have to."
"But I want to," I tell him.

sulking

The highlight of
the after-church coffee hour
is Mr. Gray.
Everyone wants him to feel
comfortable and welcome.
Especially Mavis Moon.
"Listen to her chirping
about her old cat," says
Maymee, who is sulking
by the coffee urn.
And then we hear
Mr. Gray tell Mavis:
"I have a cat too—Olive.

I brought her with me
from Michigan."

after coffee hour

The pastor
and Officer Downey are
in the church kitchen
washing coffee mugs.
Mom is wrapping
leftover cinnamon rolls.
Maymee snatches a package.
She hurries over to Mr. Gray,
who is halfway out the door.
She chirps as birdily
as Mavis Moon:
"Here's a goody bag, Mr. Gray."
Mr. Gray smiles at Maymee.
"Call me Harlan," he says.
Was that a wink?
Maymee turns to me.
"Birdie, see if Mrs. Bloom has a book on cats."
"You don't like cats," I remind her.
"People can change," she says.

I look around for Martin.
He's nowhere to be found.

on the way home

On the way home from church,
Mom drops me off at Nina's.
Nina's dad gives me a smile.
"So nice of the church," he says.
"Sammy loves the cookies."
"Martin came already?" I ask.
"About twenty minutes ago."
"So—is Nina here?"
"Nina's off with Martin. Something about
doing homework together."
Oh.

over at martin's

Martin and Nina are in
the Stefanos' backyard.
They're sitting side-by-side
at the picnic table.

They're eating chips.
Sipping lemonade.
Nina's eyes are all sparkly.
Her face all smiles.
Martin goes in to get
an extra glass for me.
"Doing homework?"
I ask.
Nina nods. "I was having trouble
with my math."
"I would have helped you,"
I tell her.
"Yeah—well, you were still
at church."

smiling

An hour goes by.
It's nearly two o'clock—
our Sunday dinner time.
"I guess I'd better go," I say.
Nina smiles. "See you, Birdie."
Martin smiles. "Bye."
I leave the two of them.

Sitting side-by-side.
Eating chips.
Sipping lemonade.
Smiling.

smiling 2

I smile back.
I'm probably the official champ of smiles.
No one can feel sorry for a smiler.
I smile all the time at school.
Even when someone in the lunch line
grabs the last slice of pizza.
I smile when I lose a favorite pen.
And on bad hair days.
When other kids talk about their dads—
or head to the art room to make
Father's Day presents—
or roll their eyes at how embarrassing
their dads can be sometimes—
I nod and I smile.
Sometimes I smile so much it feels like
my face will crack and my smile will
fall to the floor
in a thousand pieces.

gone

Once, Nina said
she understood
about my dad
being gone.
"My mom is gone too,"
she told me.
"When did she die?"
I asked her.
"Oh, she didn't die,"
she said. "She's
in Oregon.
Married to a
shoe salesman."
I smiled.

rude

Maymee squeals
when I hand her
the cat book I got at Mrs. Bloom's.
She flops down
in the nearest chair

and starts reading.
Mom has to
call her to
the dinner table
twice.
Maymee brings the book.
I put my arm around her.
"I thought it's rude
to bring a book
to the dinner table."
"Who told you that?"
she asks.
"You did."

checking

After dinner
Maymee makes
half a dozen calls
to check out
Mr. Gray.
"That's called stalking,"
I tease.
Maymee gives me a look.

"That's called prudent,"
she says.
"Harlan Gray
could be anyone.
A con man,
a bigamist,
a common criminal . . . "
"So," I say. "Which one
is he?"
"None.
He's a retired engineer
from Michigan
visiting family.
Just like he said."

choir info

Later
Mom makes
a call of her own.
"Double-checking
on Mr. Gray?" I smile.
Mom smiles back.
"No. Telling Fred Downey

what time choir practice
is tomorrow night."
I'm surprised.
"Since when does
Officer Downey sing
in the choir?"
"Since tomorrow."
I roll my eyes.
"Can he even sing?"
Mom shrugs.
"We'll find out."

magpie

On Monday—
because I'm on
the field day committee—
I take the second bus home.
Loretta Lomax
is on the same committee,
same bus.
She's talking my ear off.
"I've decided
what I want to be

when I grow up,"
she tells me.
"A baby nurse?" I ask.
Loretta loves babies
more than anyone I know.
"No. A therapist."
"Really?"
She gives me a serious nod.
"The other night
I was flipping through TV channels,
and this therapist
was explaining how
she teaches people
to work crisis hotlines.
They save lives, Birdie!
Can you imagine?"
Before I can imagine,
Loretta chatters on
like a magpie:
"Take Charlie, for instance."
"What about Charlie?" I ask.
"Have you noticed? He's been
a real grump lately."
"Yeah. You think he has a problem?"
"If he does," says Loretta,

"maybe I can help."
She pats my hand.
"That goes for you, too, Birdie.
If you ever
have a problem,
big or small,
and you want to talk about it,
let me know.
I need the practice."

happy

When I walk in my house
Martin is there,
in the living room,
chatting with Maymee.
He hands me a feather.
"I found this," he says.
"Blue jay," I tell him.
He grins. "I thought
you would like it."
I take the feather.
And it makes me happy.

Martin.
Feather.
Happy.

monday night

I'm lying on the sofa
watching *Winged Planet*
on the Discovery Channel.
Maymee waves a bag of
ancient pink rollers at me.
"I'll give you a dollar
to curl my hair."
"You hate curls,"
I remind her.
"People change."
"*Two* dollars," I say.
Maymee mutters:
"Highway robbery."

funny

I'm rolling
Maymee's last curler
when Mom comes in
from choir practice.
Late.
"Rough practice?" I ask.
Mom nods. "Learning a
new piece."
Maymee asks: "How's
Fred's voice?"
"Fine," says Mom.
"Funny," says Maymee,
"him deciding to
join the choir
after all these years."
Mom grins.
"Funny—you wanting
curls again
after all these years."

rare

On Wednesday
while I'm at school
and Mom's at work,
Maymee invites
Harlan Gray to tea.
She has him
all to herself.
"We clicked right away,"
she tells us at supper.
"So—you like him," says Mom.
Maymee giggles.
(Maymee's giggles are about
as rare as ivory-billed woodpeckers.)
"We may be in love."
"You can thank me," I say.
"I bet the curls did it."

picturing it

Even though
I've never been in love myself,
I'm almost positive
it doesn't happen
in a single afternoon.
Plus Maymee is like,
over eighty.
After Maymee goes to bed
I say to Mom:
"Aren't Maymee and Mr. Gray
too old to be in love?"
Mom kisses my nose.
"No one is ever too old
for love, Birdie."
"I can't picture it," I say.
"Try," says Mom.
Later, I try.
I close my eyes.
I can't do it.
I give up.

lovely

Harlan Gray has invited
Maymee and Mom and me
to Crab Night at Schooner's.
He arrives at the house
with three bouquets:
pink carnations for Mom and me
and yellow roses for Maymee.
Maymee floats down the stairs
in her swishy green dress
and a silvery, shimmery scarf
(*my* silvery, shimmery scarf,
which she did not ask
if she could borrow).
Harlan steps forward
and gives Maymee the roses.
"You look lovely," he tells her.
Maymee beams . . .
shimmery, like the scarf.
We head out the door
and into Mr. Gray's car.
I whisper to Mom:
"I think I can picture it now."

brownie

Martin and his family
are at Crab Night too.
Martin and I
bump into each other
at the dessert buffet.
We both reach for
the last brownie.
Martin grabs it first.
And then he laughs.
And then he gives it
to me.

early

On Saturday
I set up
the Scrabble board
two hours early.
It's my turn
to choose a theme.
The word "dating"
pops into my head.

Don't be weird,
I say to myself.
I choose
"friendship."

that's okay

At quarter to two,
Martin calls.
"I can't make it,"
he tells me.
"Are you sick?" I ask.
"No—just that Charlie and I are helping
Nina's father
paint lawn chairs.
I thought we'd be
finished by now."
I take a breath.
"Sorry."
"That's okay," I say,
then—"Bye."
It doesn't feel okay.
It feels totally
not-okay.

Not at all.
But why?
It's just a dumb Scrabble game.

nina's phone call

It's Memorial Day.
No school.
Nina calls me.
"Coming to the parade?"
she asks.
"No."
She doesn't bother to
ask why.
She just says:
"Okay, Birdie.
We'll miss you."
And hangs up.

parades

When Dad was alive,
parades used to be fun.
Mom and I got to ride
on Dad's red fire truck.
We wore matching sunglasses.
We waved little flags.
We tossed Tootsie Rolls to the crowd.
I hate parades now.

invitation

Maymee is wearing
red, white, and blue
and fluttering around
like a flag.
Mr. Gray is wearing
one of those
old-timey straw hats
with a red, white, and
blue band.
They invite me along
on their Memorial Day date.

"No thanks," I say.
"Strawberry waffles at
the diner," coos Maymee.
"No thanks," I say.
Mr. Gray gives a pout.
"But Birdie, I got up
at dawn
to set a blanket
right under a big oak tree.
We'll be in the shade."
"That's nice," I say.
He tries singing:
"Everybody
loves a parade."
I walk away.
"Not everybody."

invitation #2

Mom is on the phone.
When she gets off,
she turns to me.
"Officer Downey
invited you to

ride in his car
in the parade."
I boggle.
"Huh?"
"He thought it
might be fun."
I am hopping mad.
I growl, "Mom, you know
I don't do parades."
She gives me her
sad smile, her
I-know-how-you're-feeling
smile.
"Maybe it's time you
start liking them
again."
"Maybe it's time people
stop bugging me,"
I say and head
to my room.

long day

Memorial Day drags.
I glue bird pictures
on my charts.
I organize my closet.
I eat half a jar
of Nutella.
I read the article
that Mrs. Bloom
clipped for me
about the extinction
of passenger pigeons.
I watch a video
about hummingbirds.
I make a note
to tell Maymee
that some hummingbirds
die in their sleep.

changed

Maymee is a
changed woman.
She used to
say cats are "sneaky creatures,"
but now she shops for Mr. Gray's cat Olive:
toy mice, scratching post, cat treats.
She hasn't spoken about
funerals,
coffins,
or cemeteries
for days.
She still uses
her canes,
but there's a
definite bounce
to her walk now.
I ask Mom if
she has noticed.
"Yes," says Mom.
"It's odd," I say.
Mom tweaks my cheek.
"It's love."

man around the house

Mr. Gray is here almost
every day now.
Not that I'm complaining.
He seems truly interested in
my bird charts.
He asks a lot of questions
about birds.
He even gave me a necklace
with a silver hummingbird.
I tell Mr. Gray how
when Martin and I
play Scrabble,
we choose themes.
Mr. Gray suggests
a few themes
we haven't tried:
poetry,
aviation,
the 1940s.
He makes the best
mac and cheese
from scratch.

He helps me with
my science homework.
I help him wash his car.
I say to Mom: "I sort of
like having a man
around the house."
Mom gives me a look:
"Really?"

bomb

Mom latches on
to my remark
about having a man around the house.
"I'm glad
you feel that way, Birdie."
And then she drops
the bomb.
"Because Officer Downey and I
are seeing each other."

seeing each other

My brain knows
exactly what Mom means—
but I turn my back on it.
"Like just friends, right?" I say.
"Church? Choir practice? Right?"
"Well, more than friends, Birdie."
I don't like where this is going.
"But you hardly talk to him
when he stops by.
And he's never even taken
you on a *date*."
I think I'm squeaking.
"We've gone on dates," she says,
way too calmly.
"Aha!" I say. "All those times
you were late."
"Not always," she says,
looking a little guilty now. "But maybe
sometimes."
I jab my finger at her.
"That's the sneakiest thing
I ever heard!"

think of it

I'm too mad to stay
in the house.
I leave.
I slam the door.
Hard.
I go to Nina's.
I tell her about
Mom and Officer Downey.
Nina smacks her forehead.
"What were we thinking?"
"Huh?"
"Birdie, we could have
set your mom up
with my dad.
We could have been
sisters!"

friday evening

Mom apologizes.
And apologizes.

She tries to
butter me up
with chocolate chip pancakes
for supper.
I'd rather eat mudpies.

I go to fill in
my bird chart
and realize the only bird
I noticed today
was Tweety Bird
on my juice glass.

book return

Like most Saturdays,
I head to Mrs. Bloom's.
This time to return
a book from Maymee called

Sonnets from the Portuguese.
They're love poems.
Old ones.
Maymee has totally given up
mystery novels.
In spite of my bad mood,
I drop hair from my brush
along the way.
I pass Charlie's house.
He's lugging boxes
into his garage.
"Hey," I say.
He looks at me.
He says nothing.
Weird.
Charlie's usually good
for at least a couple words.
I keep walking.

I ring Mrs. Bloom's
bell. She opens the door.
"Happy June, Birdie," she says.
June? Already?
June . . .
Father's Day month.

half

At two o'clock,
Martin comes by
for our Scrabble game.
He gives me a crooked smile.
"I can only play
half a game today, Birdie.
We'll have to finish
next week."
"Huh?"
"I'm helping Mr. Faull again.
He needs me at 2:30."
I slap the board shut.
"Half a game is stupid."
Martin leans over.
He tugs my ear.
"Half is better than none,"
he says.
I swat his hand away.
He tries to look guilty.
"I'm sorry, Birdie.
Next Saturday—
the rest of this game
and a whole long

new one.
I promise."
I open the door
to let him out.
"Don't do me any favors,"
I tell him.

skipping sunday school

On Sunday,
Officer Downey is not
in church.
I wonder (hope)—
did he and Mom break up?
But then Mom tells me
that he will be coming over later.
My mood goes dark.
After the sermon,
I skip Sunday school
and head to our car.
I figure it's less of a sin
to think dark thoughts
in a car
than in a church building.

what i'm thinking

I'm not a monster.
I don't wish for anything
horrible
to happen to Officer Downey.
I just wish he'd get transferred
to the North Pole.
Or decide to become a monk.
Or remember he already has a wife
and twenty kids
in Brazil.
Or get hives and discover he's
allergic to twelve-year-old girls.
Because—c'mon—if my mom
had to pick only one of us—
Officer Downey or me—
she'd pick me.
Slam-dunk.
Right?

a chance

Maymee and Mr. Gray
are taking Olive to
the Cute Cat Contest
in Gillette.
I ask Mom if I can go.
She says no.
I whine: "But I've never been
to a Cute Cat Contest before."
Mom sighs. "I told you, Birdie,
Fred is coming over.
He wants to talk to you."
I flop on the sofa.
"What if I don't want to
talk to him?"
Mom sits beside me.
She leans her head
on my shoulder.
"Just give him a chance.
Please."

gift

Officer Downey taps at
the door,
then waltzes in
like he owns the place.
He gives Mom a big grin.
Then he hands me something—
all wrapped and ribboned
like it's my birthday.
Mom pokes me with her elbow.
"Open it, Birdie."
I do.
It's a pair of binoculars.
Expensive ones.
The kind I've been wanting.
"For your bird-watching,"
he says.
"It's not bird-watching,"
I snip at him.
"It's birding."

really?

Mom looks me in the eye.
"When you receive a gift,
a thank-you is always nice."
"Thanks," I say.
Hah.
Gift?
Really?
How dumb do
they think
I am?
I know a bribe
when
I see one.

whose life?

Mom asks Officer Downey
if he'd like some iced tea.
"I'd love some," he says.
Mom heads to the kitchen.
Officer Downey turns to me.
"I know it won't be easy, Birdie.

Me being in your life."
In *my* life?
Is he kidding?
He can be in Mom's life
if that's what she wants.
But mine?
Not on this planet.

a fact

I really want to
go to my room,
but that would leave
Mom alone with
Officer Downey.
So I stay.
Mom brings a tray of
iced tea and cookies.
Three glasses.
"Not thirsty," I say.
Officer Downey turns to me.
"So, Birdie," he says.
"I hear you're reading a book
about kestrels."

"Uh-huh."

"Anything interesting?"

"No."

Mom glares at me.

I cave.

"Well—one thing."

"What's that?" Officer Downey asks.

"Kestrels can see mouse pee."

after a while

I can't stand sitting here any longer.

"I'm going *birding*,"

I tell them.

I do not take the binoculars.

I do not go birding.

I go to Nina's.

She's not home.

I go to Martin's.

He's not home.

I head back to our place.

I hear Mom laughing.

It sounds different.

Brighter.

Like the way she laughed
before Dad died.
I veer away.
Okay—maybe it's time to try therapy.

clients

I walk three blocks
to Loretta's house.
I ring the bell.
Loretta opens the door.
Charlie Deale is right behind her.
He walks past me.
"Hey, Birdie," he says.
He turns back. "Thanks,
Loretta." And walks off.
"What's that all about?" I ask her.
"Sorry," she says. "Can't
talk about my clients."
"I saw Charlie yesterday," I tell her.
"He didn't even say hi.
What's going on?"
Loretta taps her lips.
"Confidential," she says.

it could be worse

I blurt out:
"My mother's seeing somebody.
Officer Downey.
I'm not happy about it."
"It could be worse," she says.
"Your mom could be dating
a real warthog."
I roll my eyes.
"Or a total cornflake.
Or a cuckoo bird."
I give a half-smile.
"You're not sounding
much like a therapist,"
I say.
Loretta gushes on:
"Or a mud frog.
Or a lemon-faced lizard.
Or a weeny string beany."
We both giggle.
It feels good to laugh.
Until I start to
cry.

crying

Loretta gets all
flustered.
"Don't cry," she says.
I blubber:
"I don't think a therapist
would tell her client
not to cry."
Loretta pulls her chair
closer to mine.
"You're right," she says.
"I'm still learning.
Cry all you want."

cat lady

By the time
I return home,
I'm all cried out.
Officer Downey is gone.
And Maymee is back
from the Cute Cat Contest.
She's wearing

cat earrings,
cat socks,
and a T-shirt that reads:
I don't care who dies
in a movie
as long as the cat lives.
"Boy," I say, "talk about
a change of heart."
Maymee acts all innocent.
"What do you mean?"
"Cats," I tell her.
"You used to hate them."
Maymee scowls.
"I never really hated cats.
I just didn't know any."
Mom pats Maymee's hand.
"And now you know Olive."
"Cutest cat ever," says Maymee.
She holds up
a blue ribbon.
"And she got first place
to prove it."

snarl, scowl

I'm still upset about
Mom and Fred.
At school on Monday
my locker door jams.
I kick it.
Charlie sees me, says:
"Move over—
I'll kick it too."
"Get lost," I snarl.
Nina breezes by,
gives me a play-bump with her elbow.
I scowl. "Ouch!"
I am definitely
no longer the
school champion
of smiles.

yes

I muddle through.
Classes.
Lunch.

More classes.
Field day meeting.
Second bus home.
Martin is waiting
at the bus stop.
"Wanna talk?" he asks.
And yes.
I do.
Yes.
Definitely!

hope

Martin and I walk to
the edge of the woods
by the creek.
We sit on a rock.
Martin faces me.
I think:
How blue his eyes are!
Like sky.
I wonder why
I hadn't noticed before.
"So," he says,

"I hear you're not happy
about your mom
dating Officer Downey?"
"Yeah," I say.
Martin gives me a crinkly grin.
"Aww—he's not such a bad guy."
"Yeah," I say. "In
somebody *else's* world."
"Are there wedding plans?"
"Yikes! I hope not," I squeal.
Martin laughs. "If there *were,*
you'd know it."
Martin's older sister Lynn
got married last year.
I remember Martin complaining
about all the fuss.
"I guess they're just dating
for now," I say.
Martin brushes a tiny leaf
from my hair.
"Don't worry, Birdie.
A lot can happen.
They can get tired of
each other.
That happened to Lynn and

her first serious boyfriend."

Tired of each other.
Something to
hope for.

not yet

After dinner, Nina calls.
"You know," she says,
"just because your mom
loves Officer Downey
doesn't mean *you* have to."
"It's not love," I say. (I hope.)
"It's just dating."
And then I give a snort.
"And even if it were love—
no way is Officer Downey going to
weasel his way into
my heart.
Like, ever."

my heart

In bed that night,
I hold my favorite picture.
I say: "My heart is yours, Dad."
And then
I think of Martin's
blue eyes.
And how he brushed the leaf
from my hair.
"Well—maybe somebody else gets
a little piece too,"
I say.
Then, like always:
"Goodnight, Daddy."

all week long

1.

Officer Downey tells me to
call him Fred.
I don't call him anything.
I never start a conversation.

I just reply if he says something
to me,
to be polite.
And so I don't get into trouble
with Mom.

2.

After Officer Downey gave me
those binoculars,
I left them on the table.
Mom put them in my room
by the window.
"You'll be able to see
lots of birds close-up
with these," she smiles.
I fake-smile back.
Then I stick them
under a stack of sweaters
at the back of
my closet.

3.

I am extra-nice to Mr. Gray,
since he's not trying to

take my dad's place.
He teaches me the jitterbug—
a dance from
the old days.
Officer Downey offers to
teach me to salsa dance.
"No thank you," I tell him.

When Mr. Gray makes
popcorn balls,
he invites me to help.
And I do.
When Officer Downey
invites me to work with him
on a thousand-piece puzzle,
I pass.

When Mr. Gray tells
a funny story,
I laugh until I get the hiccups.
When Officer Downey tells a joke.
I shrug and say, "I don't get it."

4.

At school,
my heart is a hummingbird
whenever I see Martin.
Our Saturday Scrabble game
seems eons away.

5.

Each night,
I do my bird charts.
I wear Dad's glasses.
I hold Dad's photo.
And I wonder—
does he know about us?
About Maymee and Harlan?
Is he surprised at Maymee finding
love so late in life?
Does he know
how I feel
about Martin?
Does he know that Mom
and Officer Downey are
dating?
Is he sad?
Can you be sad in heaven?

ready for scrabble

At last it's Saturday!
I change into my blue shirt.
Martin mentioned once
that blue was
his favorite color.
I set up the Scrabble board.
I've got the topic:
"friendship."
I'm as jittery as
a spring flicker.
Martin will be here
any minute.

the doorbell rings

I jump from the chair.
I bang my knee on
the table leg.
I take a deep breath.
I open the door.
It's Martin.

It's also
Nina.
Wearing a
blue shirt.

i thought

I gape at Nina.
"I thought you said
word games are
boring."
Nina shrugs.
"I changed my mind."

no enthusiasm

There was a time
when it would have been
fine with me
if Nina joined
our Scrabble games.
But that time is gone.

Like my excitement
to play
this game.

pretzel nuggets

Mom set out
cheese and
pretzel nuggets for us.
Nina flicks nuggets
at Martin and giggles.
Martin flicks one
back at her.
"C'mon you two," I huff.
"You're making a mess."
Nina pops a nugget
into her mouth.
She lays tiles down to spell
KISS.
Next turn she spells
HUG.
And then she tries
ROMANCE.
But she spells it

with an *S*.
"Wrong!" I say.
"It's a *C*.
Plus—*romance* isn't
friendship."
"It *can* be," she says.
I'm this close
to shoving
a pretzel nugget
up her nose.

next time?

Nina wins the game.
I come in last.
Nina shrugs.
"Better luck next time,
Birdie."
Earth to Nina:
there won't be
any
next time.

game over

Nina gets up.
"I have to go," she says.
Martin starts putting
the game away.
I figure he'll stay awhile.
He always does.
Then he says:
"Wait a sec, Nina.
I'll walk you home."
They leave
together.
I watch from the window.
Martin and Nina
are running
like little kids.
Laughing.
Are they holding hands?

brick

I go to bed early.
I don't bother
bird-charting.
Or brushing my teeth.
Or even putting on
Dad's glasses.
When Mom comes in
to say goodnight,
I pretend to be asleep.
My heart is a brick.

sleepless

I can't sleep.
I smack my pillow.
I shove it off the bed.
Finally I get up
and go to my computer.
I search "heartsick."
Pages and pages of
quotes come up.
Even one from the Bible,

Proverbs 13:12:
"Hope deferred
makes the heart
sick."
Tomorrow
I won't go to church.
I will tell Mom
I am too sick.
It won't be a lie.
The Bible says so.

all morning

Mom believes me.
She's staying home
and passing up a chance
to see Officer Downey.
She fusses over me—
ginger ale,
vegetable broth,
mint tea,
foot rub.
She reads an article
about bird migration

aloud:
"How Far Will Birds Go?"
(The bird with the longest
non-stop flight—
over seven thousand miles—
is the bar-tailed godwit.)
Then Mom says:
"Try to nap, Birdie."
My eyes are hardly closed
when the doorbell rings.

voices

I hear Nina.
And Martin.
They are asking Mom
about me.
They are asking
if I'm up to practicing
the sack race
or the beanbag toss
for field day tomorrow.
We are on the red team.
Martin,

Nina,
and me.
Ha!
I have no intention
of going to school tomorrow.
And if I were
(which I'm not)
I'd ask Ms. Franco,
our gym teacher,
if I could switch
to the blue team.

field day morning

I tell Mom I'm still sick.
I clutch my stomach.
"I don't think I can
make it to school."
"Okay," she says.
"Get dressed.
We're going
to the doctor."

well enough

I can't go to the doctor.
Dr. Bernstein will figure out fast
that I'm not really sick.
I get dressed.
Mom brings me a cup of tea.
I try to smile.
"Honestly, I think
I'm feeling a little better now."
"So then," Mom says,
"you're well enough to go to school?"
"Yeah—but look—"
I point to the clock.
"I missed the bus."
Mom pats my cheek.
"Don't worry,
I'll drive you."

both

Mom drops me off at school.
I march straight to
the nurse's office.

Ms. Alvaro, the school nurse,

looks up from her desk.

"Birdie, my dear,

I was just thinking of you."

"Huh?"

"I finally got hummingbirds at

my feeder this morning.

Three of them!"

"Nice," I say.

She sets her papers aside.

"All ready for field day?"

"Not exactly," I tell her.

"Why not?"

"I don't feel well."

Ms. Alvaro takes me by

the hand and leads me

to one of the cots.

"Headache? Tummy ache?"

"Both," I say.

especially

Time can't drag any slower
than when you are
flat on a school cot.
Especially if you aren't
really sick.
Especially if you're
a liar.
I play word games in my head.
I try to think of a bird
for each letter of the alphabet:
albatross . . .
bluebird . . .
chickadee . . .
dove . . .
egret . . .
fly-catching warbler . . .
Ms. Alvaro opens the window.
"Some fresh air," she says.
Field day sounds gust in.
Shouts.
Laughter.
Cheers.
If I were a bird,

I would fly out
that window
and keep going.

not that sick

Ms. Alvaro takes my temperature.
It's normal. Duh. Drat.
She fills a paper cup with ginger ale.
"Sip this," she says, "while I call your mom."
"She works on Mondays," I tell her.
"She may want to come get you."
"But I'm not *that* sick, Ms. Alvaro.
Just not up to field day."
Ms. Alvaro tweaks my chin.
"Okay, Birdie. But if you throw up,
I'm calling your mother."

at lunch time

Ms. Alvaro offers to share
the chicken soup
in her thermos.

"Thanks," I say, "but I have
my cheese sandwich.
Besides—
I don't eat birds."

red team

After school,
Nina runs up to me
in the bus line.
She's wearing a gold
plastic medal
around her neck.
"Where were you, Birdie?
Martin and I were worried."
Martin and I.
The words prick
my heart.
Martin was my friend first.
Nina points to her medal.
"Red team won!"
"Big whoop," I say.
Nina gives me a look.
"I was sick

in the nurse's office
all day," I explain.
Nina drapes her arm
around me.
"Oh Birdie, I'm sorry.
Are you okay now?"
I shrug.
"Well," she says,
"You're still a red teamer."
She whips out another
gold medal.
"Martin and I made sure
to get one for you."

plan

Mom is at her computer
when I get home.
I see
that she is
doing a lesson
and not chatting
with the Downey person.
She smiles at me.

"So, Birdie, you made it
through the day."
"Just barely," I sigh.
"Poor baby," Mom says.
And then— "We need to plan
Father's Day."

a nice moment

Every Father's Day,
Mom and I go to
the cemetery to visit
Dad's grave.
It's two and a half hours there,
two and a half hours back.
It takes planning.
What music do we listen to
in the car?
What gifts should we bring
to set by Dad's stone?
Which blanket for our picnic?
Which food to pack?
I go over to Mom.
I sit on her lap,

lay my head on her shoulder.
"Love you, Mom," I say.
"Love you too, Birdie."

the week goes by

1.

At school I avoid
Martin and Nina
whenever I can.
I spend lunch breaks
helping Ms. Alvaro
file worksheets
for the next school year.

2.

On Wednesday,
Mr. Gray has
a dizzy spell
halfway through
a movie matinee.
Maymee drives him
home.

She wants him
to see Dr. Bernstein.
Mr. Gray says
all he needs is a nap.

3.

Friday is
the last day of school.
The PTA treats
all the students
to ice cream.
The mayor of Hadley Falls
gives a speech he calls
"Summer Safety."
On the bus,
I sit next to Loretta Lomax.
Aisle seat.
Martin and Nina
sit together
across from me.
Martin leans over.
He says: "About
tomorrow's Scrabble game—"
I give him my best "who-cares"

look.
"Oh, didn't I tell you?"
I say.
"I decided I'm bored
with Scrabble."

4.

Loretta turns to me.
"Have you seen the Andersons' baby lately?
Her name is Lily.
She's so adorable!
I'm going over there after dinner.
Maybe Mrs. Anderson will
let me hold her."

5.

"That's nice," I say,
just to hear myself talk.
Because sometimes
that's what I do
when I'm sad.
I talk and talk at Loretta
like a kookaburra,
which is good,

because
kookaburras
don't
cry.

early sunday morning

I'm up before Mom.
I turn to Dad's photo and say:
"Happy Father's Day, Daddy."
I go out to fill the bird feeders.
Then eat a bowl of cereal.
Soon, Mom appears.
She's wearing the dress
that was Dad's favorite:
white with yellow daisies.
She wears it every Father's Day.
It still fits.

set to go

Last night we packed
our picnic lunch.
We put the blue blanket
in the car.
We chose gifts to bring.
Mom is bringing a stone
with the word "courage"
carved into it.
I'm bringing a tiny
ceramic owl.
We've decided to play
Christmas music
on the drive down to the city.
Christmas was Dad's
favorite holiday.
Maymee wakes up
before we leave.
She hugs us both.
She says:
"Blow a kiss
to your daddy
for me, Birdie."

here

Willow Valley Cemetery
isn't grim or spooky
like movie graveyards.
And though I wish
with all my heart
that Dad wasn't here,
at least it's pretty.
Leafy green trees,
pink roses trailing,
stone walls,
fresh-cut grass,
birdsong.
Mom and I walk to
Dad's grave.
We spread the blanket.
We sit side by side.
Mom takes my hand.
"Your girls are here,"
she tells Dad.
I blow a kiss.
"And that's from Maymee,"
I say.

remembering

Mom and I eat our cheese sandwiches.
We trade memories of Dad.
Mom tells about the time
she was in a bad mood
and Dad made pancakes
in the shape of hearts.
I tell about the time
I had a cold
and had to miss
Lorie O'Leary's birthday party,
and Dad came to my room
and said: "Want to learn
the elephant dance?"
Mom giggles. "I don't
remember that."
I stand up to demonstrate.
Feet—*thump, thump, thump*—
right arm in front of my face—
swinging it like an elephant's trunk.
Mom stands up.
We do the elephant dance together.
I think how good it is,
Mom and me doing the elephant dance.

Dad maybe watching us from heaven.
So—why do we need anyone else?

into the summer

1.

Time crawls.
Martin and Nina
ask if I want to
watch a movie.
"No thanks."
Go for a milkshake?
"No thanks."
Take Nina's little brother,
Sammy, to the park?
"No thanks."

2.

I hang out
with Loretta.
We visit the Anderson baby.
Loretta brings along
an old copy of

Johnny Tremain.
She tells Mrs. Anderson:
"Be sure to read to
Lily.
Reading aloud
will stimulate her
developing senses."

3.

I'm doing nothing
on the porch.
I notice Charlie walking by.
I've been doing nothing
for the past two hours.
I'm desperate.
"Hey Charlie," I call.
"Wanna play Scrabble?"
"Not in the mood," he says
and keeps walking.

4.

Mom is working extra hours.
(Or so she claims.)
On Friday I don't bother

to come out of my room
except to grab a bag
of pretzels.
Maymee knocks on my door.
She asks why
I'm acting so mopey.
I tell myself: *No . . .*
keep your mouth shut . . .
you can't tell her.

And then I do.

from under my nose

I go on and on about Martin.
His blue eyes.
Playing Scrabble,
just him and me.
Talking to him about my problems.
Silly things he says.
And sweet things.
I tell Maymee how Nina
stole Martin right from
under my nose.

Martin was supposed
to be *my* first boyfriend.
Maymee doesn't say
what I expect her to.
She doesn't say
you're too young for boyfriends.
She doesn't say *there are*
plenty of fish in the sea.
Instead, she says:
"Did Martin know
all this before Nina stole him
right from under your nose?"

not in so many words

"Of course not," I say.
"How was I supposed to tell him?"
Maymee makes a face. "Well—
not in so many words."
"So," I say, "how did you
let Mr. Gray know
you wanted to date?"
"I told him straight out."
I give Maymee a look. "Now I'm

confused. I thought you said—"
Maymee grins. "It's different
for people our age.
We don't have time for games."

old hat

When I was seven,
my dad gave me
an old hat of his.
"This is your
thinking cap," he told me.
"Wear this whenever
you need to think
something through."
I sure wish I had
that old hat now.
So I could think through
how to tell Martin
I want to date him
in not so many words.

my idea

I cut out a pink
paper heart.
I print:
B. B.
and
M. S.
with a drawn heart
in between.
I tuck it into an envelope.
I address it: "To Martin."
I walk over to Martin's house.
I'm about to put the note
in his mailbox
when I hear someone
call my name.
It's Nina.
"Hey," she says.
I slip the envelope
back into my pocket.
"Hi," I say.
Nina asks: "Whatcha doing?"
"Looking for birds," I tell her.

wishing

I clomp home
all sulky.
Nina ruins
everything.
I wish she
had never left
Idaho.

in no mood

Fred Downey's cruiser
is parked in our driveway.
I am in no mood
to be nice to him.
I start walking away.
Mom calls after me:
"Birdie—come here."
Can this day get any
worse?

worse

Maymee's Mr. Gray
is in the hospital.
He had a stroke.

tears, hands

"Does Maymee know?" I ask.
Mom nods. "She's at the hospital now."
"Is Mr. Gray going to be okay?"
"We don't know," says Mom.
"Can we go see him?"
"Not yet. Maybe tomorrow."
My eyes fill up.
Tears spill.
I brush them away.
Officer Downey takes my hand.
Squeezes it.
I don't pull it away.

news

It's dark when
Maymee gets in.
She looks pale
and exhausted.
She tells us that
they have stabilized
Mr. Gray.
That's the good news.
The bad news is
he can't talk,
or use his left side.
It's numb.
And worst of all—
as soon as the doctor
feels that
Mr. Gray can be moved,
his son
is coming
to take him back
to Michigan.

hospital visit

1.

On Wednesday,
Mom and I visit Mr. Gray.
He still can't move his left side.
He still can't talk.
But he gives us a lopsided smile.
Somehow it's sweet.

2.

Maymee sits by his bed,
holding his hand.
Every now and then
she raises it to her lips
and kisses it.

3.

We don't stay long.
Maymee follows us
to the elevator.
She tells us that Mr. Gray
is going to be discharged
tomorrow.

4.

"That's good news," I say. "Right?"
Maymee bursts into tears.

the word

Mr. Gray's son has come
to take him back to Michigan.
Michigan isn't the other end
of the earth.
Maymee can get there
now and again.
But it won't be the same
as their being together
every day in Hadley Falls.
I remind Maymee
that Mr. Gray was only supposed
to be in Hadley Falls
for the summer, anyway.
Maymee tells me that he thought
he might stay on.
That they had started using
the m-word.
Marry.

the next friday

Mr. Gray is back in Michigan.
His son phones.
He tells Maymee:
"The drive went fine,
but Dad is worn out."
Maymee says: "Tell Harlan I love him."
Mom touches Maymee's sleeve,
whispers:
"Tell him we all do."

day

Saturday feels silent—
kind of like the day
after Dad died.
Maymee stays in bed.
Mom brings her tea and toast.
She sips the tea.
She pushes the toast away.
All morning I try to think of
something that will
cheer Maymee up.

And then I find
the undertaker's catalog
Maymee had waved at me
weeks and weeks ago—
before Mr. Gray walked into
our church and into Maymee's heart.
I bring it to her.
"So, Maymee," I say.
"Refresh my memory.
Which of these coffins
did you like best?"

first time

For the first time
since Mr. Gray
had his stroke,
Maymee laughs.

perspective

Maymee reaches to hug me.
"Birdie Briggs, you are the best!"

"I am?" I say. "What did I do?"
"You put things in perspective."
"I did?"
"Definitely.
I can't be planning
my funeral.
I've got
a life to plan for."

plans, life

Maymee starts listing
her plans aloud:
"Go to the post office
for stamps so I can
write to Harlan
every day . . .
Shop for a new suitcase
for when I visit Michigan . . .
Check airfares."
Mom calls upstairs:
"Better get dressed, Maymee.
You've got a visitor."

visitor

There are actually
two visitors:
Officer Downey and
Mr. Gray's cat, Olive.
Maymee gives a squeak
of surprise.
Officer Downey
explains.

explanation

The original plan
was for Olive to
go back to Michigan
with Mr. Gray.
But before that
could happen,
Mr. Gray motioned for
a pen and notepad.
With his right hand
he drew a picture
of a cat.

Then an arrow.
Then a heart
with the letter *M*
in the middle.
Officer Downey gives
the note to Maymee.
"Harlan wanted
his two girls to be
together."
Maymee gets all weepy.
Officer Downey opens
the latch to
Olive's carrier.
Maymee opens her arms.
Olive scoots out
past Maymee
and darts up the stairs
and under
my bed.
Officer Downey laughs.
"Don't you love cats!"

poster

Later
the pastor's wife,
Mrs. Carey, stops by.
She brings Maymee
a poster that reads:
Love always hopes . . .
always perseveres.
"That's just what
I plan to do," says Maymee.
It occurs to me
I can do that too.
With Martin.
I can hope.
I can persevere.

Before bed,
I get out my markers.
I design my own
poster.

plan a

Olive and I have
become friends.
She spends a lot
of time
on my bed.
I spend a lot
of time
talking to her.
She's a great listener.
I tell her about
my Plan A.
"It's this—" I say.
"Tomorrow afternoon
when Nina is
on her way to
Oregon
to visit her mom,
I'll mosey on over
to Martin's.
I'll suggest
I keep him company.
I'll suggest we
play Scrabble

like we used to.
I'll bring the game along.
And the theme is going
to be cats.
I look at Olive.
"What do you think?"
Olive stretches
in the sunlight.
Lifts her head. Meows at me.
It's obvious.
She totally approves
of Plan A.

july first: evening

After dinner,
Maymee calls Mr. Gray.
"He still can't speak,
except for
garbled syllables,"
says Maymee. Then she
smiles.
"But garbled love is love too."

Officer Downey
comes by with dessert:
strawberry shortcake.
My favorite.
"Thanks, Fred," I say.
Fred?
Mom beams at me.
Fred ruffles my hair.
"You're very welcome, kid."

At bedtime,
Mom kisses the top
of my head.
"You're softening, Birdie."
I think of Plan A.
"I'm happy," I tell her.
"Well, nighty-night, happy girl."
"Nighty-night, Mom."

Just before
I drift off to sleep,
I hear the
hoo-hoo-hoo
of an owl.

Life is
good.

july second

Finally
Nina is up in the clouds
and off to Oregon.
I'm standing on
Martin's porch
with my Scrabble game.
I'm wearing my best
blue top.
It's a beautiful
summer day.
My heart is full.
I ring Martin's doorbell.
Charlie Deale answers.

hoping

"Yo, Birdie," says Charlie.
"Hey, Charlie," I say.

"Is Martin here?"
Charlie snorts.
"He lives here, doesn't he?"
I roll my eyes. "Funny."
Martin appears.
He looks happy to see me.
"Hey stranger."
"I've been busy,"
I tell him. "I brought
my Scrabble game."
"Great," says Martin.
He turns to Charlie.
"Wanna play?"
"Sure," Charlie says.
My heart sinks.
I was hoping for old times.
Just Martin and me.

cats

I set up the board.
"The theme is cats,"
I tell them.
"Cats?" Charlie exclaims.

Martin turns to Charlie: "What's
wrong with cats?"
"They eat birds," says Charlie.
He gives me a look. "Aren't
you a bird-lover?"
"Not all cats eat birds,"
I say. "Our Olive doesn't."
Charlie grins.
"Bet she would if she could."

last word

Charlie's right.
Cats eat birds.
It's nature's way.
And nature has
the last word—
right?
But hey—I'm
part of nature.
And I say maybe
somebody
ought to tell cats
how amazing birds are.

Back home,
I read to Olive
from
Birds, Birds, Birds.
"Some birds migrate at night
using the stars as guides.
During courtship, cranes
dance and sing.
Hummingbirds can fly
backwards.
Puffins fly underwater.
Blue jays bury food
for winter."
Olive blinks a few times,
then leaps off my desk
and leaves the room.
Naturally.

wednesday morning

The phone rings.
It's Fred Downey—
and it's for me.
He's built me a

screech owl nest box.
He'll be over in
an hour to
put it up.
I ask: "Can Martin help?"
Fred says: "Sure, Birdie.
The more the merrier."

cool

I dig out
the binoculars
Fred gave me
from the back of
my closet.
I hang them
around my neck.
I look at
myself in the mirror.
Birdie the birder.
Cool!

late

It would have been
really nice
to have had
the owl box
in April,
when screech owls
are nesting
and laying eggs.
But Fred is
so excited.
I don't mention
that it's too late,
that it will be months
before we can hope for
an owl.

afterwards—ice cream

Martin helps Fred
carry the big ladder
(which they used
for mounting

the owl box
in the tallest tree)
to the shed.
Then Martin suggests
that he and I
go for ice cream.
Martin orders a double cone:
moose tracks.
I order a cup of orange sherbet.
I pull money from my pocket.
Martin shakes his head.
"My treat, Birdie."
We sit on the top
of the picnic table
outside the shop.
Side by side.
Feet dangling.
My first real date.
At least it feels
like a date.
Martin puts his arm
around my shoulder.
I catch my breath.
He says, "I miss Nina.
Don't you?"

i give up

When I get back,
Maymee is reading
on the sofa.
Olive is curled up
on her lap.
Maymee takes one look
at me.
"You okay, Birdie?"
she asks.
I roll my eyes.
I throw my hands
in the air.
"I give up," I say.
And I
stomp up
to my room.

fourth of july morning

I wake up to
firecrackers going off
in someone's backyard.

People are laughing,
lugging lawn chairs
up the street
to the parade route.
The Fourth of July parade
in Hadley Falls
is always longer and livelier
than the one on
Memorial Day.
Which probably means
louder.
Like loud enough
to hear in
my bedroom,
which is why
I'll have earplugs
ready.

not the same

Mom is on the porch
hanging our flag,
chatting with Mrs. Bloom.
Maymee is at the kitchen table

eating breakfast:
blueberry-raspberry-yogurt
parfait.
Red, white, and blue.
"Yours is in the fridge,"
she tells me.
I ask, "Are you going
to the parade, Maymee?"
She shakes her head.
"It won't be the same
without Harlan."
I give her a hug.
"I know what
you mean."

later

Mom and Fred head off
to the parade.
Olive heads off
to a sunny spot
by the back door.
Maymee waters houseplants.
I rearrange my sock drawer.

Maymee washes Olive's
food dish.
I sharpen pencils.
Maymee changes a light bulb.
I fan myself with
Bird Watcher's Digest.
Maymee eats a Fig Newton.
I eat a pickle.
Suddenly parade music
whirls through
the windows.
I stuff earplugs in my ears.
Maymee turns on TV
to the shopping network,
volume way up.

my idea

I notice a tear
rolling down Maymee's cheek.
I flop beside her on the sofa.
"I miss Harlan," she says.
"I miss Dad," I say.
We sit there holding hands

while "Shopping for Zirconia"
drones on.
Then out of the blue
(maybe because
Maymee's tears
feel even sadder than
my own)
I get this crazy idea.
"Let's go to the parade!"
Maymee gapes at me.
"Really?"
"Yes!"
I yank the earplugs
from my ears.
Maymee grabs her red, white, and blue cane,
and we're out the door.

second half

Maymee drives.
We find a place to park
by the post office.
We wade through
a crowd at

the funnel cake stand.
We squeeze into
a space on the curb.
Half the parade
has already gone by.
Maymee pokes me with
her elbow.
"Second half is
always better," she says.

fire trucks and clowns

I'm okay till
the fire trucks come.
I stare at my shoes.
I swallow the lump
in my throat.
I fight the urge
to cry.
Maymee takes my hand.
She squeezes it.
Soon the fire trucks are gone.
A line of clowns appears.
They wear big, squirty rings on their fingers.

One clown marches up to me
and squirts me in the face.
Another clown grabs Maymee—
cane and all—
and dances her around.
I can't help it—
I laugh.

my turn

We don't see Fred's cruiser.
He and Mom must have
been in the first half
of the parade.
But we do see
Harlan's granddaughter,
Elena,
marching with the
Hadley Falls Organic Garden Club.
She waves to us.
My turn to
squeeze
Maymee's hand.

away

The day fills up
with root beer floats,
soft pretzels, and
flea market bargains
in the church parking lot.
I buy a mug
with a bluebird on it.
Maymee buys a yarn mouse
for Olive.
We bump into
Mom and Fred.
The four of us play bingo
in the big tent.
Fred wins an ugly
ceramic lamp.
He gives it to Mom.
She laughs. "No thanks."
Maymee eyeballs it.
"I'll take it," she says.
I decide I want a funnel cake.
Martin is there in line.
I veer away.

out of steam

Maymee fans herself
with a paper plate.
"I'm all out of steam,"
she says. "I think
I'll head home."
Mom offers to go back
with her.
Maymee waves her away.
"I'm fine. Besides—I wouldn't
want you and Fred to miss
the square dancing."
"I'll go back with you,"
I say.
Fred gives me a look.
"What—no square dancing
for you?"
I just roll my eyes.

not too bad

Maymee takes a nap.
I go to my room,

plop on the bed,
pick up Dad's picture.
I tell him:
"I went to the
parade today.
It wasn't too bad—
except when
the fire trucks
went by."

sometimes

Nina is back from
Oregon.
She brought me
a beaded bracelet.
She and Martin
hang out every day.
Sometimes they ask me
to hang out with them.
So far I've made
excuses.

sometimes 2

Sometimes
I go over to Loretta's.
She now has an office
in her basement.
She keeps begging me
to tell her my problems.
"I need practice."
I shake my head.
I don't feel like
telling Loretta
about Martin
and my broken heart.
"I don't really
have any problems right now,"
I say.
Loretta pleads
with me.
"Make some up."

sometimes 3

Sometimes
I hang out with Charlie.
One of those sometimes
we are sitting on
side-by-side swings
at the park.
I say: "You must be excited
about becoming a big brother."
"What's it to you?" he says.
I give him a look—"Well,
excuse me, Mr. Grouch—I guess
I'll just get out of here."
I slide off the swing and
start to walk away.
Charlie calls: "Birdie, hold on!"
I stop—turn. Suddenly he looks
different—maybe sad.
"I've been in
a bad mood lately," he says.
I smirk. "No kidding."
"It's because the baby's
going to be in my room.
And that means

the Legos have to go."
"So that's what you were taking
to the garage that day."
"Right."
"Bummer." Trying to
put myself in Charlie's place—
"Plus you won't be the only
kid star anymore."
"Well . . . yeah . . . maybe that too."
"And that's why you've
been seeing Loretta."
Charlie nods.
"I figured she's crazy about babies.
Maybe she can help
get me through."

busy

Maymee and I
are making cookies
to send to Harlan.
"Is Nina back
from Oregon?" Maymee asks.
"Uh-huh."

"I haven't seen her around."
I spoon the last of
the cookie dough
onto the baking sheet.
"She's been busy."
"And Martin?" says Maymee.
"He's been busy too?"
I shrug.
Maymee puts the cookies
into the oven.
She sets the timer.
"Want to talk about it?"
"No," I say.

silence

Maymee doesn't press me.
She puts the flour away.
I wipe the countertop.
She washes the mixing bowl.
I check the timer.
Silence fills the kitchen.
Not a cozy silence.
An uncomfortable one.

I cave.

"Martin likes Nina."

Maymee says: "Oh Birdie,

that's rough."

"Tell me about it," I say.

dumped

When the cookies are done,
we pack them up for Harlan
and drive to the post office.
On the way,
Maymee tells me about
her seventh-grade sweetheart,
James O'Toole.
How after only
three dates, he
dumped her for
her friend Marie.
"So what did you do?"
I ask.
Maymee chuckles.
"Well—on the day
James dumped me,

I tore up his picture
and flushed it down
the toilet."
I giggle.
"And then—" she says,
"I treated myself to
a banana split.
Extra whipped cream.
And I ate every bite.
That night
I crawled into bed
and cried myself
to sleep."
"And then what?"
I ask.
"And then I
got over it."

life

At the post office,
Maymee pulls into
a parking spot.
She turns to me.

"Years later I was
a bridesmaid at
Marie's wedding."
"Wow!" I say. "So
they got married?"
Maymee laughs.
"No. After two dates,
Marie dumped James.
She went on to
marry a fella
she met at a skating rink."
We get out of the car.
"And you married Grampy.
And lived happily ever after."
Maymee hands me
Harlan's cookies to carry.
"Pretty much," she says.
I give her a sad look.
"And then Grampy died."
She nods. "Dumped again."
We go into the post office.
"But even then, Birdie,"
she says,
"life goes on."

later

Nina and Martin
ride past me
on their bikes
together.
They wave.

Mrs. Bloom
tells me
I missed
a bald eagle
soaring past
her house.

I step in
goose poop
down by
the creek.

Olive
coughs up
a hair ball
onto one of
my favorite sandals.

Life.

Goes.

On.

. . . and on

Loretta's dad found
half a bag of birdseed
in his shed.
Loretta says
I can have it.
I go over.
We're drinking iced tea
in her kitchen.
The birdseed is on my lap.
"I hear Charlie's not too happy
about the new baby."
Loretta gives me a look:
"Who told you that?"
"Charlie," I say. "So,
do you think you're helping him?"
"I think I am."
I nod.

"Well—
if anybody can sell
the fun of babies, it's you."

. . . **and on**

Our Sunday School teacher,
Mrs. Pinski, has
volunteered us to help
with this year's
ice cream social.
Loretta and I
are in charge of
nuts and sprinkles.
Martin and Charlie
fill pitchers with
water and pour it
into paper cups.
Nina shows up.
But she doesn't
head over to
Martin's table.
Instead she
comes to ours.

She taps Loretta
on the shoulder.
"Can we talk?"
she whispers.

curious

Loretta asks
if I can manage
nuts and sprinkles
by myself
for a few minutes.
"Okay," I say.
Then she and Nina
walk to the side
of the church.
I can't wait for
Loretta to get back
to tell me what
it was all about.

confidentiality

They are gone
for more than
a few minutes.
Finally
Loretta appears.
Without Nina.
"What's up?" I ask.
"I can't tell you."
"Why not?"
"Nina's a client."
"Since when?"
"Since ten minutes ago."
"So what's *her* problem?"
"I told you before—client
confidentiality."
"Loretta, come on—
give me a hint."
Loretta covers her ears.
I'm pulling her hands away
when I hear a voice.
A boy our age
holds out a bowl of ice cream.
"Extra sprinkles, please."

the subject

I spoon three servings
of sprinkles
into the bowl.
"Thanks," he says.
I turn back to Loretta.
"Give me a hint . . . "
Loretta leans over.
"Did you see that boy?"
"Extra sprinkles?" I say.
"Yes. Didn't you think
 he looked like
an owl?"
"Huh?"
"Round glasses,
hair sticking up
all tufty . . . "
I wag my finger
in Loretta's face.
"Don't try to
change
the subject."
Loretta finger-wags back at me.
"Confidentiality."

new to hadley falls

The ice cream social
is over at two-thirty.
Loretta and I carry
nuts, sprinkles, and napkins
into the church kitchen.
Mrs. Pinski is there
washing bowls.
The "extra sprinkles" kid
is drying.
"Girls," says Mrs. Pinski,
"I'd like you to meet
Albert Evans.
He's new to Hadley Falls."

did you hear?

Outside,
Loretta jabs me
with her elbow.
"Did you hear that?
Owl-boy is *Al*, Birdie.
Get it—OWL!"

I roll my eyes.

I want to scream.

"Who cares—

forget about him.

What about Nina?"

Loretta gives my hand

a play-slap. "Give it up, Birdie."

"Is it about Martin?"

No answer.

"It's about Martin, isn't it?"

No answer.

I get in her face,

"Loretta—it's about Martin.

Isn't it!"

She looks away.

She snaps at the sky:

"Yes! It's about Martin—

it's about Nina—

they're breaking up.

She's dumping him."

oops

As soon as the words
are out,
Loretta clamps a hand
over her mouth.
"See what you made me do?
I could lose
my license!"
"You don't have a license,"
I remind her.

catching up

"Mind if I walk with you?"
It's Albert Evans,
all out of breath,
like he ran to catch up.
I'm annoyed.
I want to talk with Loretta
about Nina and Martin.
But I can't with Albert there.
Albert smiles at me.
"I heard from Mrs. Pinski

that you like birds."
Loretta laughs. "Especially
owls," she tells him.
"I'm a snail man myself,"
he says.

would i like to?

Loretta leaves us
to go to the salon
where her mom works.
Albert asks
if I'd like to meet
his pet snail, Ivan.
I would not
like to meet Ivan.
At least not today.
Today I just want to
go home and think about
Nina breaking up with
Martin and what that could mean
for me.
But then I remember
when I was new to Hadley Falls.

And how kind Martin was.
So I say, "Okay."
Albert's eyes brighten
behind his owlish glasses.
He makes a fist.
"Yes!"

nice

Ivan the snail
lives in a glass tank
with a floor of
potting soil and moss.
"Ivan likes carrots
and mushrooms,"
says Albert.
"He's cute," I say.
Albert strokes
Ivan's shell. "I found him
in the backyard.
My first friend
in Hadley Falls."
I give a smile.
"And now you

can count me as
your second friend."
Next,
Albert suggests
we look for another snail
out back.
"A friend for Ivan,"
he says.
"Not today," I tell him.
I figure I've been
nice enough
for one day.

on the way home

My mind is swirling.
Has Nina told Martin
that they're breaking up?
Will he be totally
devastated?
Also—how should
I act?
Should I make a little move?
Soon? Like today?

Or should I wait?
Should I get some advice?
From Maymee?
From Mom?
Is that a pileated woodpecker
I hear?
Or my own
beating heart?

something to tell

When I get home,
Mom is sitting
on the front porch.
I decide to ask her
for advice.
I open my mouth
to speak,
but Mom is faster:
"I have something to tell
you, Birdie."
She isn't smiling,
but there is a sly
twinkle in her eye.

something

Mom and Fred
are going to
get married.
In October.
I'm not as surprised
as I was
when Mom first mentioned
dating Fred.
And I have to admit,
I'm not as upset.
I've actually
gotten used to the idea
of Mom and Fred
together.

questions

Me: "Will we move into
Fred's apartment?
Or will he move in with us?"
Mom: "With us."

Me: "Will I have to
change my name to Downey?"
Mom: "No. You'll still be
Birdie Briggs."

Me: "Will it be a big wedding?"
Mom: "No."

Me: "Will you and Fred
go on a honeymoon?"
Mom: "Yes. The Bahamas."

Me: "Oooo . . . can I come too?"
Mom (laughing): "Definitely
not!"

distracted

By the time
I get to my room,
my head is spinning—
Mom and Fred,
Nina and Martin,
Martin and me.

And an unexpected
silly
intruder
named Albert Evans.

thinking about

Mom and Fred and Maymee
go to bingo at the firehouse.
I work on my bird charts.
I cut photos of birds
from magazines that
Mrs. Bloom gave me.
Purple martin—and I think
about Martin.
Great horned owl—and I think
about Albert Evans.
The doorbell rings.
It's Nina.
Who I wasn't thinking about.

someone else

Nina breezes in
like old times.
Like things haven't
changed between us.
And somehow,
I don't mind.
"I guess you heard,"
she says, flopping on
the sofa.
"About you and
Martin? Yes."
"From Loretta?"
"Uh-huh. She's still
learning her craft."
"Craft?"
"Being a therapist."
"I figured she'd tell."
"So how come you
broke up?" I ask.
"I like someone else."
"Who?"
"Charlie Deale," she says.

pretty funny

"Oh . . . wow . . . Charlie Deale, huh?"
"Yeah," says Nina. "He's actually
pretty funny sometimes. And Martin—
well, he's so serious."
"He is not," I say. "Martin can
be funny sometimes too."
"Fine," said Nina. "Then
you take him."

me take martin?

Shouldn't my heart
be turning
cartwheels
right now?

a present

On Monday,
Albert Evans shows up

with a present.
A game:
BirdOpoly.
"I saw it at the pet store,"
he tells me. "And I thought of you."
"B . . . b . . . but," I sputter.
"You still like birds, don't you?"
he asks.
"Yeah. But it's not my birthday
or anything."
Albert shrugs. "I was kind of
hoping you'd invite me
to play. It's like Monopoly,
only with birds."

and then

We set up the board
on the porch table.
I choose the owl
as my marker.
Albert chooses
the binoculars.
I start giving out

the money.
I hear footsteps.
I look up.
It's Martin.

choosing

"Scrabble?" asks Martin, heading
up on the porch.
"BirdOpoly." I tell him.
He eyes the board. "Can
I play?"
"Sure," says Albert. "Pick
a marker."
Martin picks the bird nest.
Why can't I
choose my first boyfriend
as easy
as choosing
a BirdOpoly marker?

serious

I'm wondering if I should mention
Nina and Martin breaking up.
Then Martin blurts: "I guess you heard—
Nina and I broke up."
"Yeah," I say. "You must be upset."
Martin shakes his head.
"Not really."
Albert pipes up: "I don't believe in dating
until high school."
Martin rolls the highest and advances to Fly.
"I agree," he tells Albert. "I liked
hanging out with Nina—but I missed
my other friends too."
Martin gives me a grin.
I can feel my face turn as red
as a cardinal.

concentrating

I try to concentrate
on the game.
But I keep thinking about

what Martin and Albert said
about not dating until
high school.
At first I'm annoyed.
Here I am trying to decide
which of them
I want to be
my first boyfriend,
and now neither one
wants a girlfriend.
And then I land on Bird Bath
and collect all the money.
And then I get to buy
Bald Eagle, Canada Goose, and
Great Horned Owl—
the best spots on the board.
And then Albert tells a joke,
and Martin and I laugh
and laugh.
And Maymee comes out with
fresh-baked brownies.
And Albert says that
after the game maybe we can
go look for another snail
in his backyard

to keep Ivan company.
And Martin says we should
play BirdOpoly
every Saturday
like we used to play Scrabble,
because he misses our games.
And all of a sudden I wonder
why I was ever
annoyed.

birthday

Dad's birthday
is coming up
in a week—
July 31st.
I ask Mom
if we will still
be making
a birthday visit
to the cemetery.
"Of course," she says.
"I'm glad," I tell her.
"I thought with

you and Fred
getting married and all . . . "
Mom pulls me into a hug.
"We are absolutely
going, Birdie.
As a matter of fact,
I've got my present
for Dad all ready."
"What is it?" I ask.
"A picture of you
filling your bird feeders."
I'm surprised.
"When did you take that?"
She grins.
"Oh—" she says,
tweaking my cheek.
"I have my ways."

my idea for dad's gift

I decide to look for
a snail to bring to
Dad's grave.
It may sound silly,

but it's comforting to me
to think of Dad having
a little company.
I'll get Albert to help.
He's a good snail-hunter.
He found a friend for Ivan.
A snail he named Lucy.
We've got all week
to search.

preparations

Maymee takes me to
the Dollar Store
to get a carrying case
for Dad's snail.
(Still looking.)
I poke holes in the lid
and cover the bottom
with potting soil
and moss.
Once Mom and I
get to the cemetery,
I will set the snail free

on Dad's grave.
For now it will need food.
I've got carrots and
mushrooms ready to go.
And a jar lid to use
as a water bowl.
Snail paradise!

group search

Martin and Charlie join
my snail hunt.
Then Loretta.
No luck.
Loretta suggests
going back to
the Dollar Store.
"Sometimes they sell
china knick-knack snails."
"No," I tell her.
"I want a
real one."

morning of july 30th

Still no snail.
Albert says he'll
keep looking
till past bedtime
if he has to.
Loretta calls.
She went to
the Dollar Store,
just in case.
"No china snails,"
she tells me.

Mom and I are
making cupcakes
to bring to the cemetery.
Fred stops by.
I'm sort of okay
with Fred now.
But this is about Dad.
And Mom.
And me.
I tell Mom she needs to
pay attention

or the cupcakes
won't turn out right
for Dad's birthday
tomorrow.
Fred takes the hint.
He leaves.

july 30th: after dinner

Albert calls.
No luck on a snail.
Loretta calls.
She says she found
a neat photo of a snail
online if I want it.
I don't.
Fred brings Mom and
Maymee home
from Dumpty's,
the new restaurant
in Hadley Falls.
They weren't
crazy about it.
Glad I skipped going.

Fred leaves.
Mom packs up
the cupcakes
for tomorrow.
She makes lemonade.
It starts to get dark.
I go out back
with a flashlight.
I start to face the truth—
Dad won't be getting
a snail for his birthday.
Fat tears roll down
my cheeks.

july 30th: just before bed

The doorbell rings.
It's Albert.
He's carrying a saucer—
and there's a snail on it.
I squeal, "You found one!"
"It's Lucy," he says.

tears

I remind Albert that
I'm planning
to leave the snail there
at the cemetery
with my dad.
"You can leave Lucy there,"
he says.
I ask him:
"What about Ivan?
Won't he be lonely?"
"I'll find Ivan another
friend," he says.
I run and get
the snail carrier.
Albert puts
Lucy in it,
gently.
Tears slide
down my cheek.
This time they're
happy ones.

july 30th: nighttime

I ask Mom about
our picnic lunch.
"All packed and
ready to go,"
she tells me.
I take my shower.
Do my bird charts.
Put on Dad's glasses
and look at the
wavy moon.
I tell Olive about Lucy.
(Do cats eat snails?)
"Don't get any ideas,"
I say.
I climb into bed.
Like always
I kiss Dad's picture.
"Goodnight, Daddy,"
I whisper. And then—
"Do I have a surprise
for you!"

a couple hours later

Something wakes me up.
Someone is in
the bathroom.
Throwing up.
I pad over
to check.
It's Mom.
She looks terrible.
She groans,
"Get Maymee.
I think I have
food poisoning."

fine

Maymee sends me
back to bed.
"I'll take care
of Mom," she says.
"What about tomorrow?"
I ask.

Mom's head wobbles when
she looks up at me.
"I'll be fine, Birdie,"
she says.
She doesn't sound fine.

surprise

I surprise myself—
I actually
fall back to sleep.
When I wake up,
the sun is shining.
It's a blue-sky day
for Dad's birthday.
I quickly get dressed.
I carry Lucy downstairs.
Maymee is in the kitchen.
The tea kettle is boiling.
She's making toast.
"How's Mom?" I ask.
"Not good," says Maymee.

fault

Maymee says that Mom
probably got food poisoning
from the potato salad
she ate at Dumpty's.
She says
food poisoning only lasts
a day or two.
She says Mom and I
should be able to
get to the cemetery
over the weekend.
I don't want to go to
Dad's grave over the weekend.
I want to go today—
on his birthday.
I can't stop thinking
that Mom would be okay
if Fred hadn't taken her
to dinner at stupid Dumpty's
yesterday.
It's all
Fred's fault.

hopping mad

I'm too hopping mad
to eat breakfast.
I'm too hopping mad
to say "that's okay"
when Maymee
says how sorry she is
that she can't drive me
to the cemetery.
(She stopped city driving
two years ago.)
I'm even too hopping mad
to cry.

upstairs

I go upstairs.
Mom's door is open,
but she's asleep.
I set Lucy's "house"
on my desk.
Olive is curled up
on my bed,

all cozy in a
puddle of sunlight.
I curl up next to her.
I hate this day.

sounds

I hear the doorbell.
I hear Fred asking
Maymee about Mom.
I hear his footsteps
on the stairs.
I slam my bedroom door.
I hear Fred talking softly
to Mom.
I hear Mom throwing up
in the bucket by her bed.
I hear Fred leave
Mom's room.
I hear a tap at
my door.
"Birdie?
It's Fred."
"I know who it is."

"Are you ready?"

"Huh?"

"I'm driving you
to the cemetery
today."

what else

There is no time to think. So I don't.
I grab Lucy.
Mom whisper-calls to me
from her room.
She gives me the picture
she took of
me filling the bird feeders.
"Blow a kiss to Dad for me,"
she says. "And don't forget
the lemonade. And the cupcakes . . . "
"And the sandwiches," I say. "I won't."
Maymee hands me a pink seashell.
"For your dad," she says.
My hands are full. I tell Fred to
get the lemonade and picnic cooler.
He tells me to get in the car.

We start driving.

Now I have time to think.

Fred Downey is taking me to

the cemetery for Dad's birthday.

I don't like it.

I wish Mom was the one going.

But what else can I do?

on the way to the cemetery

Fred tries to chat.

I'm polite. But that's it.

Fred: "So—seen any interesting
birds lately, Birdie?"
Me: "All birds are interesting."

Fred: "We can stop for ice cream
on the way back."
Me: "No thanks. I don't want to
risk food poisoning."

Fred: "Maymee tells me you've
been playing a new game."

Me: "Yeah."
Fred: "What's the game?"
Me: "BirdOpoly."

Fred: "Any cat contests
coming up for Olive?"
Me: "Nope."

Fred: "I've been thinking—maybe next spring
I could put a brick patio
on the back of the house."
Me: "That's nice."

Fred: "Guess I'll turn the radio on.
Anything you'd like to listen to?"
Me: "Not really."

at the cemetery

Fred parks
on the cemetery road
nearest Dad's grave.
He asks if I want help
carrying the stuff.

"No thanks," I say. "I'll
make two trips."
I pull the cooler and
thermos of lemonade
from the back seat.
"Darn!" I growl.
"Something wrong?" Fred asks.
"Forgot the blanket," I tell him.
Fred goes to the trunk. He gets
his blanket. "For emergencies,"
he says.
He drapes it over my shoulder.
On the second trip I get Lucy,
the photo, and Maymee's seashell.
"How long can I stay?" I ask.
Fred ruffles my hair.
"As long as you like, Birdie."

at the grave

I set things up.
Then sit on the blanket.
"Happy birthday, Dad,"
I say.

I tell him: "Mom has
food poisoning."
(I blow Mom's kiss).
"So it's just me.
And Lucy the snail."
I don't mention Fred,
who has left the car
and is sitting on the grass
beside the road,
his back against
a tree.
I'm thirsty.
I get a cup
from the cooler.
I pour myself
some lemonade.
I unwrap a sandwich.
There are two of them.
One for me. One for Mom.
Like always.
And four cupcakes.
Because we each
always eat two.

finally

I'm talking to Dad
and eating my sandwich.
I'm looking at the
gravestone—
but out of the corner
of my eye
I keep seeing Fred
over there by the tree.
I try to concentrate
on Dad,
but I can't help
wondering:
Is Fred thirsty?
Is Fred hungry?
Finally I turn.
I call:
"Hey, Fred."

introduction

Fred comes over.
He sits on

the other side of
the blanket.
I say to Dad:
"This is Fred Downey.
He's a police officer.
He sings in the choir
with Mom."
I don't say anything
about the wedding
in October.
Fred gives a nod
to Dad's gravestone.
"Here," I say.
I hand Fred
Mom's sandwich.

when it's time

I tell Fred
I'm ready to go.
Lucy is settled
on Dad's grave
munching on a carrot.
Fred gathers most

of the stuff
and takes it to the car.
I fold the blanket.
Fred comes back for me.
He says how nice
he thinks it is that
Mom and I
visit Dad regularly.
He tells me about
his dad, who died
when Fred was in college.
"I don't go to
the cemetery much,"
he says. "But I miss
him every day."
"It must be lonely—
visting your dad
all by yourself,"
I say.
I take Fred's hand
in mine.
I say:
"Next time you want to
visit your dad,
I'll come with you."

And then we walk back
to the car
together.
Me and Fred.

last week of august

A week ago, Maymee flew to Michigan
to spend time with Harlan Gray.
I drew a picture of Olive
for Maymee to give him.
She says he loves it.

And Nina broke up with Charlie.
First Martin. Then Charlie.
One summer: two dumped boyfriends.
I told Nina that maybe she and I
just aren't ready for dating.
Maybe we should just concentrate
on friendship with boys.
Mom says there's a lot
to be said for friendship.

Loretta has changed her mind

about becoming a therapist.
She wants to be a baby nurse instead.
Good thing—because Loretta is
a lot better with babies
than with other people's secrets.

And speaking of babies—
Charlie's shopping for materials.
He's going to make a toy chest
for his future baby brother.
And his dad gave him space in the garage
to set up
his Lego sets.

a sign

Last night when Albert and I
were outside on his patio
playing BirdOpoly,
an owl feather floated down
and landed on the board.
I took that as a sign
that when I *am* ready
for my first boyfriend—

it will definitely be
Albert Evans.

family

Today Mom and I are with Fred
at his dad's grave.
We've eaten our picnic lunch,
and now Fred is planting
a rosebush.
I've brought a picture
of Mom and me
in a plastic frame.
I set it by the gravestone.
I tell Fred's dad:
"We're family now,
Mr. Downey.
So you'll be seeing
a lot of us."

ACKNOWLEDGMENTS

Warmest thanks to the following who supported *Birdie* with their expertise on birds, small towns, medicine, and middle-school life:

The Glenside James girls—Natalie, Kathy, Angel, and Lana

Mary Elmore DeMott

Anne Miles DeMott

Joan Donaldson

Elvira Woodruff

Dr. Martina Martin

Ben Spinelli

And to my kind, insightful editor, Kathleen Merz, and the wonderful Eerdmans staff.

Also—and always—to Jerry Spinelli, my husband and fellow author, who keeps me under his wings.